D0352376

PET

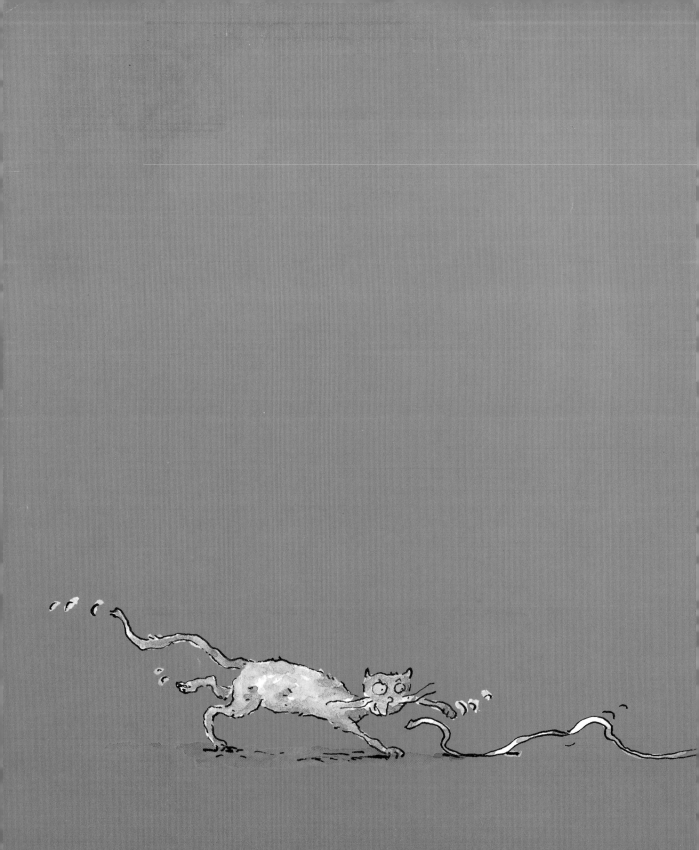

WHAT DO YOU WANT TO BE, BRIAN?

Written by Jeanne Willis
Illustrated by Mary Rees

Andersen Press • London

For my wee boy, Ruaraidh - M.R.

For Adam, Alicia and Danny - J.W.

Text copyright © 1996 by Jeanne Willis. Illustrations copyright © 1996 by Mary Rees.
The rights of Jeanne Willis and Mary Rees to be identified as the author and illustrator of this work have been asserted
by them in accordance with the Copyright, Designs and Patents Act, 1988.
First published in Great Britain in 1996 by Andersen Press Ltd., 20 Vauxhall Bridge Road, London SW1V 2SA.
This paperback edition first published in 1998 by Andersen Press Ltd.
Published in Australia by Random House Australia Pty., 20 Alfred Street, Milsons Point, Sydney, NSW 2061.
All rights reserved. Colour separated in Switzerland by Photolitho AG, Zürich.
Printed and bound in Italy by Grafiche AZ, Verona..

10   9   8   7   6   5   4   3   2   1

British Library Cataloguing in Publication Data available.
ISBN 0 86264 809 2
This book has been printed on acid-free paper

What do you want to be, Brian?

"He wants to be the greatest violinist since Yehudi Menuhin," said his mother.
"Do I?" said Brian.

"You do," said his mother and she bought him a violin and made him practise for two hours every day.

Brian tried, but the strings kept snapping and he would
keep sticking his bow where he shouldn't.

"He doesn't want to be a violinist," said his father, "he wants to be a computer wizard, like me, don't you, son?"
"Well…" said Brian.

"Of course you do!" said his father. "I've spent an absolute
mint on this new computer."

Brian did his best, but the instructions went in one ear and straight out of the other. Then the wretched thing blew up.

"He doesn't want to be a computer wizard," said his sister,
"he wants to be the most famous ballet dancer since Nureyev."

"I…" said Brian.
"Shut up and put these tights on," said his sister.

Brian really tried, but he kept dropping the ballerinas. And he accidentally kicked the pianist off her stool. And he snagged his tights.

"I'm telling you, he wants to be a boxer," said Brian's brother. "He wants to be the heavyweight champion of the world. Come on, Brian, put your mitts up."

But Brian preferred his nose the way it was.

" That lad wants to be the best jockey since Lester Piggott," said his uncle. "You want to get him a horse."

"I wouldn't bet on it," said Brian.

"Horse?" snorted his auntie. "What good is a horse when it's quite plain to me he wants to be an artist, like Van Gogh."

"He wants to be an admiral," said the vet, "like Nelson."

"He wants to be a politician!" said the man who sells
funny little brushes door to door.

"STOP!" shouted Brian. "I want to be…

"...I want to be..."

"Well, what DO you want to be, Brian?"

"I want to be the most ordinary little boy in the world,"
said Brian. And guess what …

… he was brilliant at it.

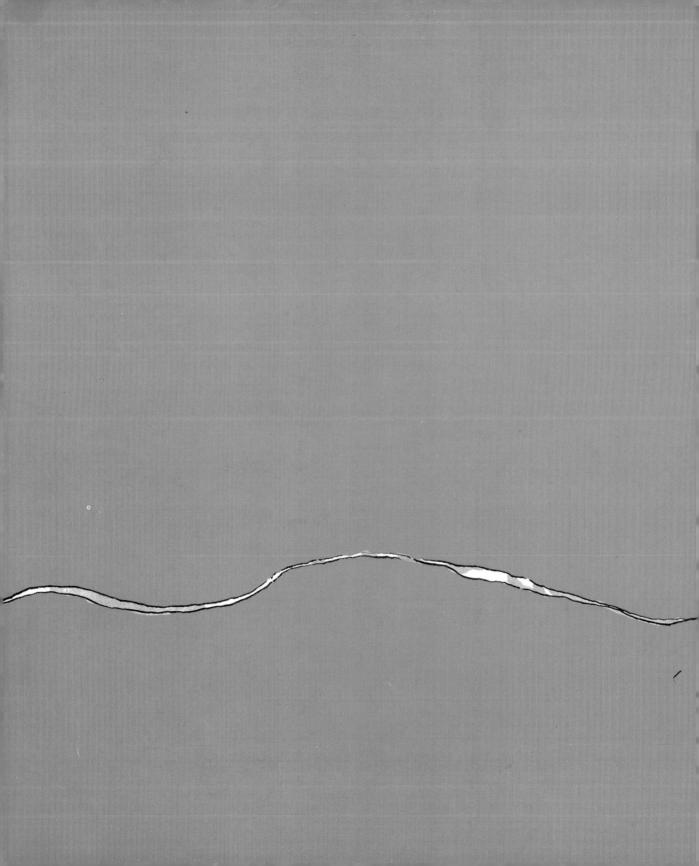